# Five reaso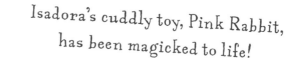 love Isadora Moon . . .

Meet the magical,
fang-tastic Isadora Moon!

Isadora's cuddly toy, Pink Rabbit,
has been magicked to life!

Pack a bag—
you're going on holiday
with Isadora!

Isadora's family is crazy!

Enchanting
pink and black
pictures

D0505123

# Where would your dream holiday destination be?

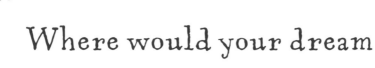

Catching a shooting star to Saturn's rings: an upside-down place full of glitter waterfalls and chocolate rain.
– Penelope

A magical woodland forest holiday with the fairies and elves in their toadstool houses and pet unicorns.
– Holly

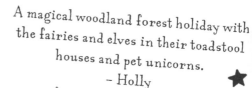

A theme park hotel with rides
and a twisty slide to breakfast.
– Annabel

I'd like to go to a rainbow. I
would stay in the violet ray.
– Tabitha

Candy land where the everything
is made out of sparkling sweets.
– Ariella

An underwater fairy sea castle
with fairy mermaids, having
parties with sea animals.
– Lena

# Family Tree

My Mum
Countess Cordelia
Moon

Baby Honeyblossom

My Dad
Count Bartholomew
Moon

Me!
Isadora Moon

Pink Rabbit

For vampires, fairies and humans everywhere!
And for Dominic, my favourite brother.

# OXFORD
### UNIVERSITY PRESS

Great Clarendon Street, Oxford OX2 6DP

Oxford University Press is a department of the University of Oxford.
It furthers the University's objective of excellence in research, scholarship, and
education by publishing worldwide. Oxford is a registered trade mark of Oxford
University Press in the UK and in certain other countries

Copyright © Harriet Muncaster 2020
Illustrations copyright © Harriet Muncaster 2020

The moral rights of the author/illustrator have been asserted
Database right Oxford University Press (maker)

First published 2020

All rights reserved. No part of this publication may be reproduced,
stored in a retrieval system, or transmitted, in any form or by any means,
without the prior permission in writing of Oxford University Press,
or as expressly permitted by law, or under terms agreed with the appropriate
reprographics rights organization. Enquiries concerning reproduction outside
the scope of the above should be sent to the Rights Department, Oxford
University Press, at the address above

You must not circulate this book in any other binding or cover
and you must impose this same condition on any acquirer

British Library Cataloguing in Publication Data

Data available

ISBN: 978-0-19-277164-3

3 5 7 9 10 8 6 4

Printed in Great Britain by Bell and Bain Ltd, Glasgow

Paper used in the production of this book is a natural,
recyclable product made from wood grown in sustainable forests.
The manufacturing process conforms to the environmental
regulations of the country of origin.

MIX
Paper from
responsible sources
FSC® C007785
www.fsc.org

# ISADORA ★ MOON

## Goes on Holiday

# Harriet Muncaster

**OXFORD**
UNIVERSITY PRESS

# Chapter ONE

'What on earth are those?' asked Dad, pointing at my breakfast bowl one grey and gloomy morning. 'They look completely disgusting!' My dad is a vampire and he only likes food if it is red.

'They're Rainbow Loopy Loops.' I told him. 'Everyone in my class is eating them. They're yummy!'

'Hmm,' said Mum, spooning some
flower nectar yoghurt into her own bowl.
'They might be yummy but they don't look
very . . . natural.' My mum is a fairy and
loves eating fresh fruit and flowers.

'Well you said I could have them,'
I pointed out. 'Yesterday in the human
supermarket you said I could have them
because I tidied my room.'

'I know,' said Mum. 'But I didn't think
you'd actually like them.'

'Mine!' shouted my baby sister
Honeyblossom from her highchair, and
reached out her hand for a Rainbow Loopy
Loop. Honeyblossom is a vampire fairy just
like me but she's not old enough for Loopy

Loops. I moved the box in front of my bowl

so that she couldn't see them any more.

Now she couldn't see me either and
I couldn't see her. Or Mum and Dad!
I munched happily on the rest of my
breakfast and stared at the back of the
box which was decorated all over with
rainbows and unicorns. One of the
unicorns was wearing a pair of sunglasses
and eating an ice cream. There was a big
speech bubble coming out from his mouth
which said:

Then there was some information below about how to enter. You had to draw a picture of your favourite teddy on the beach and then post it off. That would be fun! I could draw Pink Rabbit! I felt a shiver of excitement run through me. A family holiday! Abroad! I had never stayed in a human hotel before or been on a plane. It would be a great surprise for Mum and Dad!

As soon as breakfast was over I ran up to my bedroom to draw my picture. I got out my collection of shells from when we had gone camping and laid them around Pink Rabbit so that we could pretend we were at the beach. Pink Rabbit struck a pose and I tried really hard to copy it, sticking sequins and glitter onto my finished drawing. It took me ages!

When it was finished I put my picture in an envelope and slipped it into my schoolbag. I would put it in the postbox on my way to school in the morning.

The next day at school, I told my friends what I had done. None of them seemed quite as excited as I thought they would be.

'I've entered loads of those types of competitions before,' said Bruno. 'I've never won anything!'

'Me neither,' said Sashi.

'Don't get your hopes up Isadora,' said Oliver. 'You probably won't win.'

'Oh,' I said, feeling disappointed. My head had been so full of sandy beaches, blue sparkling seas, exciting plane rides, and colourful ice creams that the thought of *not* winning hadn't even occurred to me. But of course my friends were right. It was very unlikely. Zoe put her arm around me.

'Good luck anyway,' she said. 'You never know what will happen. I won a ten pound voucher to spend at the toyshop once!'

'Thanks Zoe.'

I smiled. But the idea of a bright and sunny holiday abroad was already starting to feel very far away and by the end of the day I had forgotten all about it.

Three weeks later I was busy painting pictures with Pink Rabbit at the kitchen table when I heard my dad come downstairs from his daily sleep.

'What's this?' I heard him say.

And then: 'What IS this? Cordelia! Cordelia, come here!' I jumped from my chair and ran into the hallway, with my mum and Honeyblossom following close behind. We all peered at the letter that Dad was holding in his hands.

'It says we've won a competition!' said Dad, looking bewildered. '*Abroad!*'

'What?' said Mum. 'They must have made a mistake. We didn't enter a competition!'

'*I* did!' I squeaked excitedly, my heart feeling as though it was about to burst out from my chest. 'I entered it. And we WON!' I couldn't believe it! Mum and Dad both stared down at me, their eyes wide with surprise.

'We're going on a plane!' I said breathlessly. 'And to the beach!'

'The beach?' said Dad, looking nervous now. 'Oh no. I can't go to the beach. It's too hot for me there. Too hot, too sticky, and too bright. No, no, no. My vampire eyes won't be able to take it!'

'It says we'll be staying in a hotel,' said Mum, sounding equally concerned. She fluttered her hands worriedly, and glittering pink fairy flour puffed into the air from the cake she had been baking. 'Do we have to stay in a hotel?' she said. 'I find them so unnatural and boxy. I'd rather camp!' But Dad had perked up a bit now.

'Is it a fancy hotel?' he asked, peering at the letter. 'Will there be a spa? There *is* a spa!'

'And I bet there will be red ice creams to cool you down Dad,' I said. 'And Mum and Honeyblossom and I can spend all day swimming in the sea and playing on the beach. In *nature*.'

'Well,' said Mum. 'That *does* sound quite nice. I suppose I can put up with a hotel for a week if I must.'

'Yay!' I shouted and then danced round both my parents until I was dizzy.

# Chapter TWO

'You can't take all that!' said Mum, gesturing at the five packed suitcases by Dad's feet on the morning of our holiday.

'I need it all,' insisted Dad. 'All my grooming products are in there. And the factor 60 sun cream.'

'They won't let you on the plane with all that,' said Mum. 'There's a luggage allowance, remember. It said so on the tickets.'

'Humph,' said Dad. 'I still don't see why we have to go on a plane. We could have gone in a flying vampire taxi!'

'But we've won free plane flights,' said Mum. 'And it will be fun to have the full human holiday experience!'

'Humph,' said Dad again, but he opened his suitcases and began to take things out, huffing and puffing the whole time.

'You don't need much for a beach holiday,' said Mum, patting her small, neatly-packed handbag. 'All I'm taking is my swimming costume, some sunglasses, and a flower crown!'

When Dad had finished condensing his five suitcases into one we left the house

and drove to the airport. I had never been to an airport before, and I felt butterflies of excitement flutter in my tummy as we neared the looming metal building.

'A monstrosity,' tutted Mum.

Through a fence in the car park I could see planes. Some weren't moving, and others were just taking off or coming in to land. I hadn't realized quite how big they would be in real life.

'Wow!' I said, staring up at the sky with my mouth open.

'Quite something!' said Dad, staring up with me. 'They do look sleek and swish don't they! Maybe I'm quite excited about going on a plane after all!'

We hurried into the airport, and to a desk where a lady wearing lots of lipstick looked at our passports and weighed our suitcases. 'You can go through to security now,' she said, as our suitcases disappeared along a conveyer belt. 'That way please,' and she pointed towards a sign that said 'Gate 23'.

'Where's my suitcase going?' said
Dad. He sounded worried. 'Will I get it
back?'

'Of course,' smiled the lady.
'You'll see it again at the
other end!'

We followed the lady's directions and walked towards another conveyer belt. We had to put our hand luggage onto it and then walk through a metal detector.

'This is a load of faff and nonsense,' said Dad, 'just to fly in the sky!' He walked through the metal detector and it beeped loudly.

'Have you got any metal on you, sir?' asked a friendly-looking man wearing an airport uniform. 'Jewellery items? A belt?'

'Of course I'm wearing a belt!' said Dad. 'My best belt! For travelling.' He opened up his cape to reveal a wide belt

with a big silver buckle on the front of it.

Around it hung many small items: a pair of nail scissors, an emergency sewing kit, a penknife, a tube of hair gel, a bottle of red juice, a blindfold, and some ear plugs.

'It's got everything I'll need for the flight,' said Dad. 'We vampires use these all the time for long distance flying.'

'I'm afraid the rules are a bit different on a plane,' said the security guard and he took away the penknife, the red juice, the sewing kit, and the scissors. Dad stared, baffled.

'I don't understand human travel at all!' he said.

We got through the rest of security and came out in a big waiting area that had lots of shops in it. While we waited for our flight Mum gave Honeyblossom her pink milk and I followed Dad into one of the shops.

'Aftershaves!' exclaimed Dad, and set about spraying himself with all sorts of different scents from the tester bottles. I joined in too, admiring all the pretty perfumes and giving them a sniff.

Suddenly there was an announcement over a loudspeaker. 'Flight number 2834 is boarding now,' it said. 'Please go to Gate 23.'

'That's us!' said Dad excitedly.

The plane seemed enormous up close and it made a loud humming sound as we stepped on board. A lady wearing shiny high heels peered at our boarding passes.

'Welcome,' she said. 'Your seats are over there,' and she pointed to a row of three seats halfway down the plane. I ran over and squeezed in, settling down by the little oval-shaped window with Pink Rabbit on my lap so that he could see out.

We could see a man down below, loading
all the suitcases into the plane.

Once everyone was sitting down,
the lady with the high heels stood up and
waved her arms about telling us where
the exits were in case of an emergency.
I noticed that Dad started to tap his foot

on the floor nervously.

'It's OK Dad,' I said. 'A plane is actually one of the safest ways to travel! Miss Cherry told me.'

'Really?' said Dad. He stopped tapping and looked a bit happier.

Then something rumbled underneath us and we started to move. I watched out of the window as we rolled along the tarmac and over to a long stretch of runway. We began to speed up, zooming faster and faster until suddenly we weren't on the ground any more. We were lifting up into the air! I stared in wonder as the ground

got further and further away, and the
buildings and cars below turned into tiny
little dots. We broke through the clouds
and I realized that I had never been so
high up before. The clouds looked like soft
fluffy blankets from above, and I wished
I could leap out of the plane to go and
bounce on them.

'Gosh!' said Mum. 'We are high! I've never flown above the clouds before! Isn't the world beautiful?'

I stared out of the window until it got too bright and then I opened up my backpack and got out my colouring book. I flipped down the little table in front of me and began to colour. A lady came round and asked us if we wanted drinks.

'Red juice for me, thank you,' said Dad, and was very pleased when the lady handed him a glass of tomato juice.

'I'm glad to see that they are equipped for vampires here,' he said.

It felt very nice to be sitting there next to Mum and Dad, high above the clouds with my colouring book, apple juice, and Pink Rabbit. I spent a happy hour colouring in and when I had finished I put my book back in my bag and poked Dad.

'Are we nearly there?' I asked.

'Nearly,' he said. 'Only another two hours to go.'

'Two hours!' I said. 'That's ages!'

Honeyblossom started to grizzle and the two hours went by very slowly. I played a game of noughts and crosses with Mum, and looked at the inflight magazine with Dad, and then at last a voice came over the loudspeaker to tell us to put our seatbelts back on because we were about to land. I watched out of the window as we went back down through the clouds and towards the blue sparkling sea and white sandy beaches below.

'Look!' I said. 'Mum, Dad, it's the sea!' Then I felt a big bump as the wheels of the plane hit the tarmac of the runway, and in front of us stood another airport gleaming silver in the bright sunshine.

'Right!' said Mum once we were off the plane and had got our suitcases back. 'Time to find a taxi!' We made our way out of the airport and into the bright sunshine outside.

'My eyes, my eyes!' cried Dad, delving into his suitcase for his sunglasses and pointed black parasol.

It was very hot outside, hotter than I had ever felt before.

'Wow!' I said, stepping into the shade of Dad's umbrella. I am half vampire after all. Mum opened up her arms and closed her eyes, putting her face to the sky.

'Glorious!' she said. 'I do so love the

sunshine. Summer fairies are like flowers you know!'

'Quick!' said Dad, as sweat began to pour down his face. 'Let's get into a taxi.'

He stuck out his arm and hailed one and we all bundled into it. Immediately Dad got out the factor 60 sun cream and began to slather it on.

'You too Isadora,' he said. 'It's our only protection!'

The taxi moved off and I looked out of the window at our surroundings. The buildings all looked different from the houses at home and there were palm trees all along the side of the road.

'How lovely!' exclaimed Mum.

The taxi stopped outside a large hotel, in front of a beach.

'Here we are,' said Mum. Dad leapt out and scurried up the steps of the hotel to stand in the shade of the doorway. It was much cooler inside the hotel and there was a big reception desk at the side of a circular room with a marble floor. A nice man helped us carry our suitcases upstairs and showed us to our room.

'This is very nice!' said Mum. 'And look at the view!'

'I can't look at any more bright things,' said Dad, lying down on the bed and putting his hand on his forehead. 'My poor vampire eyes need to rest.'

'Can we go to the beach?' I asked, jumping up and down. 'Please, please, please?' I ran to open my suitcase and

began pulling on my swimming costume.

'Look!' I said. 'I'm ready!'

'All right,' Mum laughed. 'We'll go to the beach and Dad can stay here for a rest. Dad peeped out with one eye from behind his hand.

'I might go to the spa,' he said weakly.

# Chapter
# THREE

Mum, Honeyblossom, and I made our way
out of the hotel and across the road to
the beach. It was covered in sunloungers
and umbrellas. There were food stalls
nearby too, so Mum bought us some lunch
and an ice cream. We found a nice spot
on the sand and put our towels down. I
licked my ice cream and wriggled my toes

in the warm sand while Mum changed

Honeyblossom into her swimming

costume.

'Isn't it nice Mum!' I said.

'It's lovely Isadora,' said Mum. 'Well done for winning the competition.' But there was a tone to her voice that made me think she wasn't completely happy. I stared round at all the people on the beach, lying on their sunloungers, playing, and eating snacks. There were a lot of them. Maybe it was too busy here for her.

'Shall we go swimming?' Mum asked. 'Come on, the sea looks sparkling!' She picked up Honeyblossom and we made our way over to the crystal clear water, stopping to pick up an old empty crisp packet that was lying on the sand.

'Such a shame,' tutted Mum, as she scrunched it up to put in the bin later.

We paddled into the sea and splashed about for a while. I put on my snorkel and dipped my head under the water so that I could see little silvery fish darting about, and twirly pink shells lying on the ripply sand. I could see something else too—a plastic ring with a little dinosaur on it. I reached out and grabbed it, holding it up in the air for Mum to see.

'Look!' I said. 'Treasure!' Then I slipped it onto my finger and admired it in the sunshine. Mum looked a bit troubled.

'It's not really treasure,' she said. 'It's litter.'

Just then we heard the sound of music coming across the water and we turned round to see a big boat floating on the sea. There were people in it who looked as though they were having a lot of fun. The boat came in near to the beach and stopped. Some of the people began to jump off the sides of the boat making big splashes in the water. Then I noticed a slide coming off the back of the boat. People were whizzing down it into the water, shrieking and laughing. On the side of the boat was a big sign saying: 'BOOK YOUR TOUR NOW'.

'Can *we* go on the boat' I asked Mum. 'Please? Dad will be able to come. He can stay in the cabin.'

'I don't see why not,' said Mum. 'We can book it when we get back to the hotel.'

'A boat ride?' said Dad, looking dubious. He was lying on the big double bed in our room with two cucumber slices on top of his eyes.

'Yes!' I said. 'We've booked onto it for tomorrow!'

'It looks like a nice tour,' said Mum. 'The boat is going to take us round all the little beaches and islands nearby.

I'm hoping to see some unspoiled scenery.'

'I don't know . . . ' said Dad. 'I've already got a massage and a face peel booked for tomorrow at the spa.'

'Oh please come Dad!' I said. 'I want to show you how good I've got at underwater swimming! And don't worry about the sunshine. You'll be able to stay in the cabin.'

'Well . . . all right,' said Dad. 'I suppose I don't want to miss out on a trip with my family. And I would so like to see your underwater swimming Isadora.'

The next morning after we had eaten breakfast at the hotel we made our way along the road to the place where the boat was docked. A friendly man in a pirate hat showed us on board. We were offered brightly-coloured drinks with sticks of fruit and shiny umbrellas in them.

'Yum!' I said.

'Mmm!' said Dad, sipping at his own bright red cocktail. When all the people had come aboard, the engine started to rumble and we were off! I ran up to the

top deck and peered over the railing at the
twinkly aqua blue sea below.

'This is the life!' said Mum, closing her eyes and letting the wind ruffle her wild pink hair. We soon stopped in a deserted little cove a little way down the coastline, and I watched the man in the pirate hat drop the anchor into the sea. Then everyone started jumping in and swimming about in the clear, glassy waters.

'Just what I was hoping to see!' smiled Mum, gazing at the cove with its rugged rocks and beautiful white sand. 'Some unspoiled nature!'

'I want to go on the slide!' I yelled, racing towards the back of the boat and leaping onto it. 'Wheee!' I went all the way down and SPLOSHED into the sea.

'Good job Isadora!' called Dad from the cabin window. 'I might have a dip myself!' I trod water and watched as Dad came whooshing down the slide too.

'How refreshing!' he said, and he began to do a fast front crawl around the boat. I followed him, splashing in the

waves and holding my breath so that I
could dip my head under the water.

It was like a different world—
everything was blue and hazy. I could
see the legs of all the other people
moving about in the water and the
dark shadow of the boat on the sand.

And there was something else too, something shimmery moving about behind a rock in the hazy distance. It seemed familiar. What could it be? I didn't want to swim too far away from the boat so I climbed back up the ladder and to the top deck of the boat where I peered into the ocean below.

It was hard to see anything with the sun reflecting off the water so I shook my wings dry and then flapped into the air and over to the rock which was a little way away. Peering behind it I could see the shimmery thing again. It was glimmering and glittering. And it was coming up towards the surface of the water!

My heart started to beat fast, and I
flapped my wings and rose higher into the
air as the thing burst up in a shower of
salt and scales.

'Isadora!' it cried. 'I thought I
recognized you!'

It was Marina the mermaid! I had met Marina once before when we had been on a camping holiday by the beach, but that had been much nearer to where we live.

'Marina!' I said. 'What are you doing here?'

'I was going to ask you the same thing!' said Marina.

'We're on holiday,' I said. 'I won a competition!'

'We're on holiday too!' said Marina. 'How funny!' She laughed, and it sounded like strings of shells tinkling in the breeze. 'It's nice to see you again!' she said. 'Where's Pink Rabbit?'

'He's on the boat,' I said. 'He doesn't like the water.'

'Oh yes,' said Marina. 'I remember.'

'Where are you staying?' I asked. 'I didn't know mermaids went on holiday!'

'Of course we go on holiday!' said Marina. 'We like to visit warmer waters every now and then. There are mermaid hotels in different parts of the sea all over the world you know.'

'Really?' I gasped. 'I'd love to see one!'

'Maybe I can take you underwater again like last time,' said Marina, and her eyes started to twinkle. I could give you another seashell necklace to help you breathe underwater! You can come and meet my mum and dad! And my new pet sea unicorn!'

'A sea unicorn?'

'Yes, it's like a seahorse but a unicorn! She's called Ocea.'

'OH-SHA,' I repeated. 'That's pretty!'

Marina nodded happily. 'I think Ocea and Pink Rabbit would get on,' she said. 'You should definitely visit. How about tomorrow? Where are you staying? I could come and meet you at the beach?'

'We're at the Hotel Magnificente,' I said, 'round at Pearl Cove.'

'Ah yes,' said Marina. 'My parents and I swam there yesterday to explore. It's very busy isn't it? We didn't stay long;

there were too many people and too much
rubbish lying under the water. It made us
sad.'

'I guess it is very busy there,' I said,
scrunching up my hand so that Marina
couldn't see my dinosaur ring. 'Is there
really a lot of litter under the water then?'

'Yes,' said Marina. 'Unfortunately. We tried to clear some of it away but we can't take it up to the land. We don't have legs!'

'Oh . . . ' I said. 'But I have legs! Why don't I come and help? You could pass the rubbish to me and I could take it up to the beach to be cleared away.'

'That sounds like a great plan!' said Marina.

Just at that moment I heard my name being called from the boat. 'Isadora! Where are you?' It was Mum and she sounded panicked. Quickly I poked my head up from behind the rock and waved.

'I'm here!' I called.

'What are you doing all the way over

there?' shouted Mum. 'Come back now please, the boat's about to leave!'

'OK, coming!' I yelled. Then I turned back to Marina. 'I have to go,' I said. 'But when can we meet again?'

'Wait there a minute!' said Marina, and dipped down into the sea, coming back up with something in her hands. It was a big conch shell.

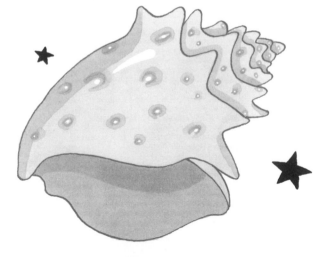

'You can use this to talk to me!' she said, holding it out for me to take. 'Just put it to your ear. You'll hear the sea!' Then she waved goodbye and with a flip of her pink tail disappeared back into the water. I flapped my wings and flew back over to the boat.

'What were you doing?' said Mum when I landed on the deck. She sounded a bit cross. 'You should never, ever disappear off without telling us where you're going! Especially when we're in a foreign country, or in a dangerous place like the sea!'

'I'm sorry,' I said. 'I forgot.'

'We were very worried for a moment,' said Dad.

'I know,' I said. 'I'm really sorry. I
won't do it again, I promise!'

## Chapter FOUR

For the rest of the day I kept the shell close to me, hoping that Marina would call. At last, when I was snuggled up in my hotel bed with Pink Rabbit snoozing beside me, I heard a whispery little voice coming from inside the shell.

'Hello!' it said. 'Isadora! Are you there?'

'I'm here!' I whispered excitedly,
pulling the covers over my head and
hoping that Mum and Dad couldn't hear
me. They were brushing their teeth in the
en suite bathroom.

'Isadora! I've got
a problem!' came Marina's
voice. 'I need you to come quickly!'

'What problem?' I asked, my heart
starting to beat fast.

'There's no time to explain!' said
Marina. 'I need you to bring your wand!
Can you come?'

'Er . . . ' I said, starting to panic. I
knew that Mum and Dad would never let
me go out to the beach on my own but
Marina sounded desperate.

'I don't know,' I said.

'Please!' begged Marina. 'I've found
a baby turtle but he's stuck! I need your
fairy magic!'

'Oh no!' I said, immediately jumping out of bed. I couldn't bear to think of a poor baby turtle in trouble. I stuffed my pillow under my duvet to make it look as though I was still in bed with Pink Rabbit and then sneaked past the bathroom door and out of the room, half running and half flying down the stairs of the hotel. It wasn't long at all before I was on the beach and peering out to sea, trying to spot Marina.

It felt strange to be there in the dark and quiet. There were no people about and all the sunloungers had been stacked away. The sand shone bright and white under the light of the big full moon. Suddenly

there was a rippling in the water and a head popped out into the moonlight. It was Marina!

'Hello!' I called and flew over to where she was bobbing in the sea.

'Thank goodness you came!' said Marina. 'Thank you!' She held out a pearly shell necklace for me to put on.

'Like last time,' she said. 'It will help you breathe underwater!'

I slipped the necklace over my head and followed Marina, sinking down into the inky blackness of the sea. The further down we went, the lighter it seemed to get. All around us jellyfish shone with their own iridescent light and the coral on the seabed seemed to glow. But as I gazed around at our beautiful underwater surroundings I saw that something was not quite right. There were things glittering and shining amongst the seaweed and shells on the seabed. But they were things that were not meant to be there. I could see an empty tin can, an old plastic cup, a lid from the top of a sun cream bottle, a long piece of fishing wire waving in the current. None of this was treasure; it was litter. Marina swam over to a clump of seaweed that was jerking about and gently parted it.

'Look!' she said. Among the fronds was a tiny baby turtle stuck in a tangle of fishing wire.

'I just can't untangle it!' said Marina. 'And it's too tight to cut! The line is already digging into his leg.'

I felt my whole throat tighten. It was horrible to see such a beautiful creature looking so helpless. I took my wand out from my pocket and waved it in the water. Bubbles streamed out and covered the little turtle, breaking the fishing line in the places where it was tight around his legs. As soon as he was free, the tiny turtle began to paddle upwards, swimming round and round in a circle, a little lopsidedly.

'I think his leg is still hurt,' said Marina. 'The fishing wire must have been very tight!' She reached out and scooped up the little turtle, holding him close to her chest.

'Let's look after him,' she said. 'Until his leg is better. Let's take him back to the mermaid hotel. You can meet Ocea!'

'I'd love that!' I said. Together we swam deeper into the sea until we came to a building fashioned completely from shells and decorated all over with pearls. Marina led me inside, past a desk with a mermaid sitting behind it and down a winding corridor.

'This is our room,' she said, pushing

open a door and motioning for me to
follow her. 'These are my parents!'

A mermaid and a merman were
both sitting on a huge shell-shaped bed.

The merman was reading a copy of the *Underwater Times* and the mermaid was busy brushing her hair. Bobbing round both their heads was a small sea unicorn who came dashing over to nuzzle Marina as soon as she entered the room.

'Hello Ocea!' said Marina, patting her gently. 'Mum, Dad, this is the friend I was telling you about. This is Isadora Moon!'

'Isadora!' said the mermaid and stopped brushing her hair immediately. 'We've heard a lot about you.'

'We have,' said the merman. 'Jiggling jellyfish! I've never met a vampire fairy before! Do come in!'

I followed Marina into the room and

watched as she put the baby turtle gently down onto her bed. Ocea the sparkling little sea unicorn came swimming up to me, blowing star-shaped bubbles out into the water. Marina's mum made us some sea tea and put some octopus-shaped biscuits on a plate.

'Isadora says she can help clear away the rubbish on the seabed,' said Marina.

'That's great!' said Marina's dad. 'We could really do with some help from someone with legs!'

'I *think* I can help,' I said, munching

on one of the biscuits. It was delicious, if a bit damp.

'What do you mean?' asked Marina.

'Well,' I said. 'I didn't realize how much rubbish there is! I think we might need more help than just me.'

'Oh,' said Marina's mum sounding worried. 'Who can we ask? We can't trust the humans!'

'My mum and dad!' I said. 'I'm sure they would love to help! I'll ask them tomorrow!'

# Chapter FIVE

The next morning at breakfast I told Mum and Dad all about Marina and her family.

'Fancy!' said Dad. 'I didn't know mermaids were still about!'

'Of course they are,' said Mum. 'I used to frolic with mermaids all the time as a young fairy, whenever we visited the beach!'

'Did you?' I said in surprise. 'I didn't know that!'

'Oh yes,' said Mum. 'I had a mermaid penfriend back in the day. I used to write her letters on waterproof paper. But never mind that for a moment. Isadora it was very wrong of you to sneak out in the middle of the night without telling us!'

'Yes,' agreed Dad, looking stern. 'We already told you that yesterday!'

'I'm sorry,' I said. 'I really didn't mean to do it again. Marina needed my fairy magic!'

'It was very kind of you to help the turtle,' said Dad. 'But you should have asked us to come with you. It can be dangerous to go out on your own. How did you get back in to the hotel?'

'I flew through the window,' I said.

'Hmm,' said Mum.

'I was just so worried about the turtle,' I said, 'I didn't think properly.'

'Well,' said Mum. 'Just don't do it again! Or I will confiscate your wand for a week!'

'I won't,' I promised. 'I really won't! So will you come and help clear up the ocean tonight?'

'Of course!' said Mum. 'We'd love to!'

That night, Mum, Dad, Honeyblossom, Pink Rabbit, and I stood on the beach and waited for Marina and her parents to appear.

'So much nicer to go to the beach at night,' said Dad, 'without all that horrible sunshine!'

'I like the sunshine,' said Mum, 'but I do agree that it's much more peaceful right now without all the people.'

We waited for a few more minutes and then a little splash appeared in the ocean and three heads bobbed up out of the water. We flew over to them, waving.

'Hello!' called Mum. 'It's lovely to meet you!'

'And you!' smiled Marina's parents. Marina handed Mum and Dad a special shell necklace.

'Put them on,' she said, 'and you'll be able to breathe and talk underwater!'

'Will it stop me getting wet?' asked Dad. 'I've only just gelled my hair into the perfect flick!'

'I'm afraid not,' said Marina. Pink Rabbit started to look worried. He hates getting wet.

'Pink Rabbit can go inside a bubble,' said Marina, and splashed about in the water until it frothed with bubbles. Then she put one on her finger and blew on it so that it got bigger and bigger.

'Mermaid magic,' she said with a wink.

'Humph,' said Dad. 'I don't see why

I can't have a bubble too!' But Marina and her parents had already dipped back down under the water.

I sank down too and began to swim, following Marina and her parents into their magical underwater world.

'It's stunning down here!' said Mum, and her hair waved about her like the tendrils of a pink sea anemone. 'But I can see your problem. There's rubbish everywhere! Such a shame!'

'It is!' said Marina's mum. 'But I think we can all do something about it. I'm going to get all our mermaid friends to help too. We'll gather up all the rubbish and bring it to you above the surface. Then you can fly with it back to land. It's going to be a big job and will probably take us the rest of the night.'

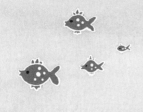

'That's OK,' said Dad. 'I'm used to being awake during the night.'

'And I'd do anything to help our beautiful planet,' said Mum.

Mermaids and mermen began to appear, bringing huge nets with them to collect up all the litter that was lying on the seabed.

'I can't believe the things people throw away,' said Marina, picking up an old, soggy trainer and trying to force the end of her tail into it. 'I do find shoes funny.'

'Humans just leave things on the beach,' said Marina's mum, picking up an old, deflated rubber ring, 'and then it gets washed away. I don't think they realize where it goes.'

'We need to tell them!' I said.

'*We* can't,' said Marina. 'But maybe you could?'

When enough of the rubbish had been collected, Mum, Dad, and I began to fly it to shore. We laid it all out on the beach and as the night wore on it grew into a huge pile, getting bigger and bigger and bigger.

'Well,' said Mum, when we had done
as much as we could. 'People are going to
have to take notice of this!'

'They will,' I said, thinking about what Marina had said. The sun had started to peep over the horizon now and I knew the humans would start to wake up soon. We flew back to the sea where Marina and her parents were bobbing with their heads poking out of the water.

'Thank you so much for your help,' said Marina's dad. 'We couldn't have done this without you.'

'The seabed looks so clean and beautiful now,' smiled Marina's mum. 'The fish are happy!'

'Well let's hope it stays that way,' said Mum.

I gave Marina a salty seawater hug.

'Maybe I'll see you again?' I said.
'We'll be staying here for the rest of the
week!'

'Definitely,' said Marina. 'I'll call you
on the shell phone!'

# Chapter SIX

Mum, Dad, Honeyblossom, Pink Rabbit, and I made our way back to the beach. Early morning risers had started to appear and they were standing, gazing up at the mountain of shining plastic and metal.

'Where's it come from?' asked a man who was wearing a shirt with pink flamingos all over it.

'I just can't imagine!' said a lady in a big striped floppy hat.

'Well it certainly spoils the landscape,' said someone else.

'It does, doesn't it,' agreed Mum.
And she began to tell the people about
how all the rubbish had been cleared
up from the seabed and I followed her,
telling everybody who would listen about
the little turtle that had got stuck in the
fishing wire.

'But that's awful!' said a little boy in
turtle-patterned swimming shorts. 'I love
turtles!'

'Me too!' said a lady in a pink bikini.
'Years ago there used to be loads of them
swimming round this beach.'

'Maybe they'll come back now the
rubbish has gone from the sea,' said Mum.

'I hope so!' squeaked the little boy,

jumping up and down with excitement.

'Maybe we could put up signs?' said one of the hotel owners who had come outside to investigate. 'To remind people not to leave litter lying about.'

'And to recycle!' said someone else.

'I think that would be an excellent plan,' smiled Mum. 'Nobody's perfect but we could all try a bit harder to look after our world.'

More and more holidaymakers were starting to come down to the beach now, and a few people were bringing wheelbarrows to cart away some of the rubbish to the recycling centre. Suddenly there was a shout and the lady in the pink

bikini started jumping up and down and
pointing at the water.

'Look!' she said. 'Look!'

In the sea were three big, beautiful
turtles all happily swimming about.

'Wow!' yelled the boy. 'Amazing!
Amazing!'

'Just breathtaking,' said the man in the flamingo shirt. 'Let's hope we are able to keep it clean enough for them to stay.'

'Isn't nature incredible,' sighed Mum. I jumped up and down with excitement and then ran back into the hotel to our room to find my shell phone tucked under my pillow. I wasn't sure how to work it but I put my mouth to the opening and said 'Marina! Marina?' Then I put it to my ear and listened to the *woosh, woosh* of the sea.

'Yes?' came a whispery voice a few moments later.

'It's me!' I said. 'I was calling to ask about our turtle. I think I've found some friends for him! How is he? How's his leg?'

'Much better today,' said Marina. 'He's swimming about happily in our hotel room and I've been taking him up for air. Sea turtles can only hold their breath for a few hours at a time you know. It was lucky that we found him in the fishing wire when we did!'

'It really is!' I said, feeling sick at the thought of what might have happened.

'I think he's ready to be set free now,' said Marina sounding sad. 'I'll miss him.'

'Let's do it together,' I said. 'Tonight, when the beach is quiet.'

'All right,' said Marina. 'I'll see you then.'

This time I made sure to tell Mum and Dad what I was planning to do.

'We'll watch from the hotel window,' said Mum. 'To make sure you're safe.'

That evening, once everyone had left the beach, I went down there in the moonlight and waited for Marina to appear. It wasn't long before the water rippled and Marina's head popped out. She was holding something in her cupped

hands. It was our baby turtle! He looked
so much better now. And happier too.

'I saw some other turtles swimming
in the bay earlier,' I said. 'Big ones!'

'Really?' said Marina. 'That's great
news!'

'Hopefully our turtle can go and
join them,' I said. 'Can I hold him to say
goodbye?'

Marina gently tipped the turtle into
my own cupped hands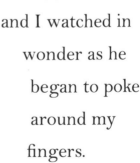
and I watched in
wonder as he
began to poke
around my
fingers.

'Good luck little turtle!' I whispered.

'You can let him go,' said Marina, 'if you want.'

I lowered my hands into the water and let the tiny turtle swim off them.

He seemed surprised at first to be out in the open waves but then excited. He began to paddle away from us, keeping his head close to the surface of the water. I watched as he swam further and further away, his shell shining in the moonlight.

'I hope he'll be OK,' I said, as he disappeared into the distance.

'I'm sure he will,' said Marina. 'I'll make sure the mermaids here keep an eye on him! And hopefully the humans will keep the sea clean too. That's the most important thing.'

We both smiled at each other and I thought about what an exciting holiday it had been so far. And there were still five days to go!

'Shall we meet again tomorrow?'
I asked.

'Definitely!' said Marina and
splashed her tail with glee. Tiny droplets
sprayed into the air and sparkled like
diamonds in the starlight.

'I'll call you on the shell phone,'
she said.

Turn the page
for some
Isadorable
things to make
and do!

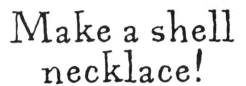

# Make a shell necklace!

Next time you go to the beach, why not collect some shells and turn your favourite ones into a necklace?

## Method:

1. Search for shells with holes in them.

2. Take the best ones home and wash thoroughly.

3. Thread on to a piece of string.

4. If you would like to, add beads, pompoms, or any other decorations.

5. Tie the two ends of the string together (making sure it's long enough to fit over your head!)

6. Make some more for your friends!

# Keep a holiday journal

Remember all of the fun things you did on holiday with a holiday journal! You can either buy a scrapbook to stick things in to, or staple your own pages together.

## Record your memories in whatever way you like best! You could:

1. Write down what you did at the end of every day.

2. Draw your favourite thing that happened.

3. Stick in tickets and receipts.

4. Make a photo album.

Then you will have something to always remind you of the lovely things you did!

# What is your best kind of holiday?

## Take the quiz to find out!

### What is your favourite weather?

**A.** I like it when it's hot hot hot!

**B.** I like the sunshine, but I like to shelter indoors too.

**C.** I like the rain, and I like the sun. I just like being in the great outdoors.

### What do you enjoy doing in your spare time?

**A.** Swimming.

**B.** Visiting interesting places.

**C.** Going for walks.

### What do you like to eat?

**A.** Ice cream!

**B.** I can't choose, I have so many favourites.

**C.** I like my packed lunch.

# Results

## Mostly As

You love the beach! For you there's nothing better than splashing about in the sea, playing in the sand, and having fun outside.

## Mostly Bs

You love the city! There are museums and art galleries to visit, people to watch, and lots of things to learn!

## Mostly Cs

You love the countryside! Long walks in any weather, wide open spaces, and peace and quiet are your idea of a great holiday!

# Many more magical stories to collect!

ISADORA MOON
Goes on a School Trip
Half vampire, half fairy, totally unique!
Harriet Muncaster

ISADORA MOON
Gets in Trouble
Half vampire, half fairy, totally unique!
Harriet Muncaster

ISADORA MOON
Goes to the Fair
Half vampire, half fairy, totally unique!
Harriet Muncaster

ISADORA MOON
Makes Winter Magic
Plus fun-tastic activities!
Half vampire, half fairy, totally unique!
Harriet Muncaster

ISADORA MOON
Puts on a Show
Plus fabulous activities!
Half vampire, half fairy, totally unique!
Harriet Muncaster

ISADORA MOON
Has a Sleepover
Half vampire, half fairy, totally unique!
Harriet Muncaster

Harriet Muncaster, that's me! I'm the
author and illustrator of Isadora Moon.
Yes really! I love anything teeny tiny,
anything starry, and everything glittery.

# Love Isadora Moon?
# Why not try these too...